To Carter Drury, and to Cassidy and Tyson Adams
B. W.

To Ann, one of my Paris writing pals
D. C.

Text copyright © 2006 by Barbara Williams
Illustrations copyright © 2006 by Doug Cushman

First edition 2006

Library of Congress Cataloging-in-Publication Data is available.

Library of Congress Catalog Card Number 2005058210

ISBN-10 0-7636-2097-1
ISBN-13 978-0-7636-2097-4

2 4 6 8 10 9 7 5 3 1

Printed in Singapore

This book was typeset in Horley.
The illustrations were done in watercolor, ink, and colored pencil.

Candlewick Press
2067 Massachusetts Avenue
Cambridge, Massachusetts 02140

visit us at www.candlewick.com

ALBERT'S
Gift for Grandmother

Barbara Williams illustrated by Doug Cushman

CANDLEWICK PRESS
CAMBRIDGE, MASSACHUSETTS

Today was Grandmother's birthday.
The Turtle Family could hardly wait
for her to arrive.

"Happy birthday!" said Albert, Homer, Marybelle, Mother, and Father.

"Thank you," said Grandmother. She sank heavily into the easy chair.

"Mama and I baked you a birthday cake," said Marybelle.

"How lovely," said Grandmother.

"Did you bring us some gummy worms?" Homer asked.

"You shouldn't ask Grandmother for presents on her birthday," said Marybelle. "You should be giving presents to *her*."

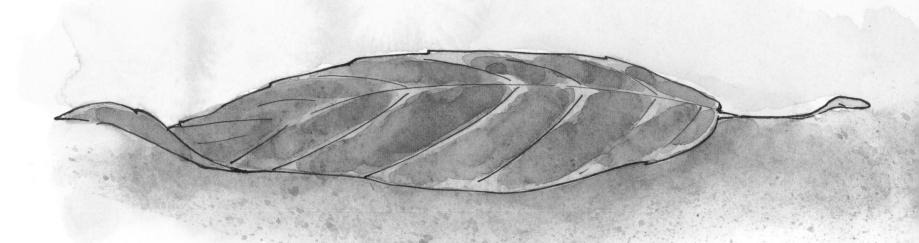

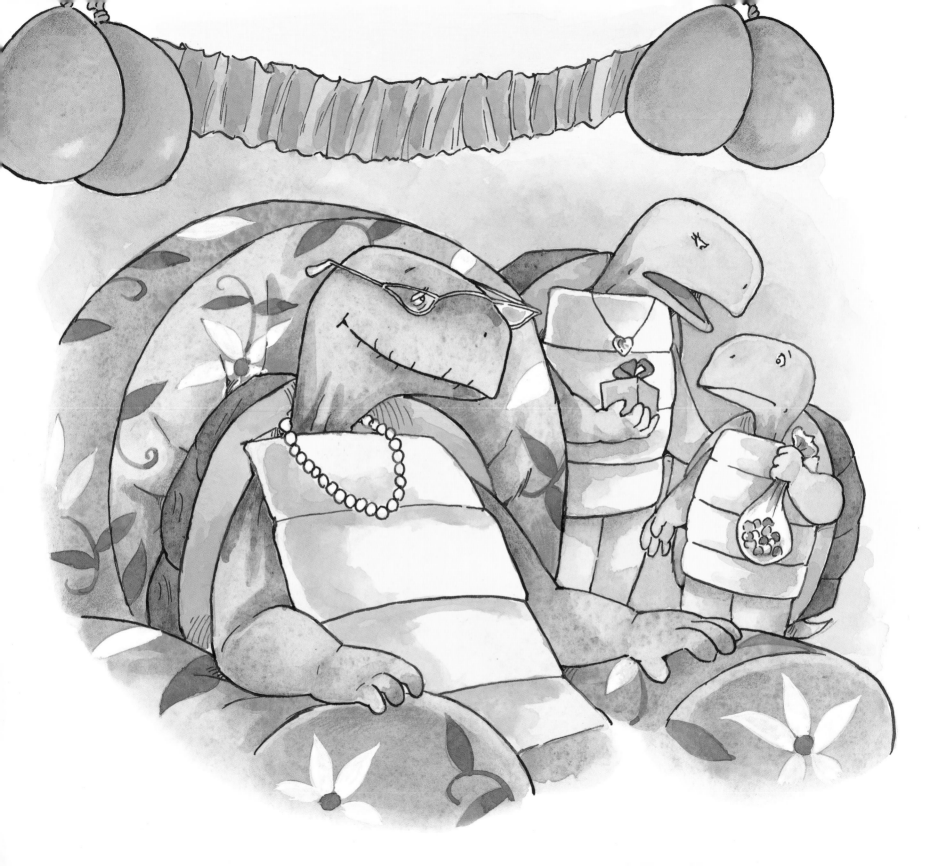

Albert had been planning exactly what his present would be.

"Come outside with me, Grandmother," he said. "I'll teach you how to play marbles for your birthday."

"Well, dear, I—" Grandmother began.

"You should give Grandmother something she can take home, like the present *I* made," said Marybelle. "Anyway, it's too cold to go outside today. Isn't it, Grandmother?"

"Yes, a little, I suppose," said Grandmother. "Will you teach me to play marbles another day, Albert?"

"Yes'm," Albert said.

"Why don't you sit on the couch, Mother?" asked Father. "Your feet don't touch the floor in that big chair."

"Oh, but it's nice and soft," said Grandmother. "I'll just stay here if you don't mind."

"All right," Father said. "You children entertain your grandmother—I'll be right back."

"Close your eyes, Grandmother, and guess what my present is," said Marybelle. "I'll give you a hint. It's pink, your favorite color."

Homer groaned. "I'll bet I know what it is. A silly bracelet."

"It is NOT silly!" said Marybelle. "See?"

"It's lovely, Marybelle," said Grandmother. "Thank you very much."

Albert wished *he* could make a bracelet for Grandmother. But he didn't have any beads.

"I have a better present for you, Grandmother," said
Homer. "I'll show you how I can skateboard. I've been
practicing some scary tricks for your birthday."

"Not too scary, I hope," she said.

"Hoo! I'm not afraid of any scary tricks! And I'm not
afraid of the cold, either," said Homer. "You can stay
inside and watch me through the window."

Homer opened the door to go outside. "I'm the best skateboarder in my class. Don't forget to watch, Grandmother!"

Albert wished *he* could show Grandmother some tricks. But he didn't know how to skateboard.

"Look at me!" shouted Homer. "I'm doing scary tricks!"

"Oh my!" wailed Grandmother.

"Your tricks are too scary!" shouted Albert.

"You're just a baby who still sucks his thumb," Homer called back. "Watch me jump again, Grandmother."

"Please don't tease your little brother, Homer," said Grandmother. "And please close the window, Albert — I'm getting a chill."

Albert wanted to hide. He went into the kitchen where Homer couldn't make fun of him.

"That's a pretty cake," he said.

"Thank you," said Mother. "It's my present for Grandmother's birthday."

Albert wished *he* could give his grandmother a cake for her birthday. But he didn't know how to bake.

Then he had an idea.

"Albert Turtle!" Mother cried. "What are you doing up there?"

"Grandmother is cold, so I want to make her a cup of hot dandelion tea for her birthday," he explained.

"Well, get down before you fall and break your shell," said Mother. "I'll fix some tea for everyone in a few minutes, when the cake is ready."

"Yes'm," said Albert.

In the living room, Albert could see that Father and Homer had both come inside. Father was showing something to Grandmother.

"I just made this footstool for your birthday," said Father. "You can use it whenever you come to our house and want to sit in that easy chair."

"Oh, that feels much better," said Grandmother. "Thank you."

Albert sighed. He wished *he* could build something for his grandmother. But he didn't know how to use Father's tools.

Albert felt sad. He was the only one who didn't have a gift for Grandmother. He wanted to get his blankie and rub it against his cheek while he sucked his thumb. But then Homer and Marybelle would tease him. And his mother and father—even his grandmother—would say he was too old to hold his blankie and suck his thumb because now he was a big turtle who went to kindergarten.

Suddenly Albert had a new idea. A wonderful idea.
He hurried to his bedroom.

When Albert returned, he was hiding something behind his back.

"I have a very special present for your birthday, Grandmother," he said. "You can take it home to keep, just like Marybelle's bracelet."

"Why, Albert, it's your blankie!" exclaimed Grandmother. "Are you sure I can take it home to keep?"

"Yes'm," said Albert. "It's your birthday, and you're cold. I don't need it anymore because I'm a big turtle now and I go to kindergarten."

"Thank you, darling," said Grandmother. "What a thoughtful, generous gift."

"Here's your birthday cake. I hope you like it," said Mother.

"Oh, it's perfect!" said Grandmother. "Just like all my gifts."

"Shall we sing Happy Birthday?" asked Father.

"And then let's eat!" said Homer.

So they did.